DISNEY PRINCESS

pi
kids ®

phoenix international publications, inc.

Dear Diary,

It's been another busy day here in the tower. With so many things to do, time just flies! After I finish painting, I think I'll write a song. Or read a book. Or maybe Mother Gothel needs a new pair of mittens? Decisions, decisions!

Rapunzel

Search far and near for Rapunzel's gear:

these vases

knitting needles

darts

this book

puzzle

puppet

ballet shoes

guitar

Dear Diary,

   What a story this has turned out to be! When I first came to the Beast's castle, I wasn't sure I would like it. But no one could ask for a lovelier home or kinder friends. As for the Beast himself—well, you can't judge a book by its cover.

Belle

Please take a look for Belle's favorite books:

Thumbelina

Fairy Stories

Romeo and Juliet

Mother Goose

The Three Little Pigs

The Princess and the Pea

Dear Diary,

Picnic day! We packed something yummy for everyone, from the Prince's favorite strawberry cake to carrots for the royal horses. And of course there was a treat—seven treats, to be exact!—for my friends the Dwarfs.

Snow White

Look for these treats
the royal horses would eat:

carrots

apple

oats

bran

sugar cubes

corn

horse treat

hay

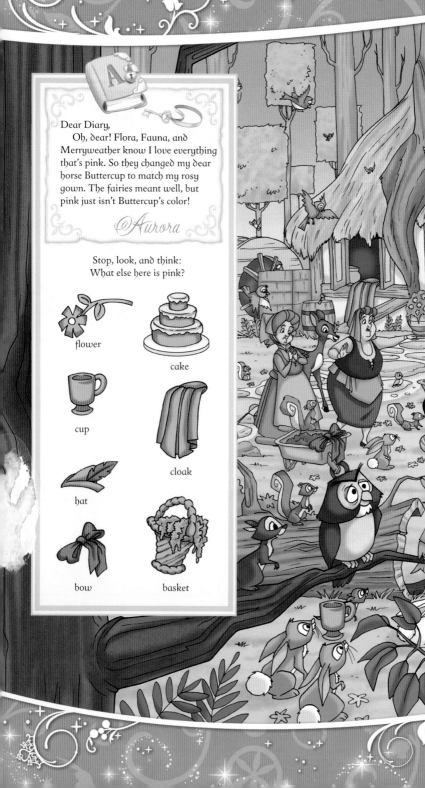

Dear Diary,
  Oh, dear! Flora, Fauna, and
Merryweather know I love everything
that's pink. So they changed my dear
horse Buttercup to match my rosy
gown. The fairies meant well, but
pink just isn't Buttercup's color!

Aurora

Stop, look, and think:
What else here is pink?

flower

cake

cup

cloak

hat

bow

basket

Dear Diary,

Today I followed the will o' the wisps to the Witch's cottage. Mum and I have not been getting along lately, and the Witch gave me a powerful spell to make things change. What did she put in it? Och, I'm not sure I want to know!

Merida

Look long enough to find this magical stuff:

mortar and pestle

this secret ingredient

tongs

welding mask

measuring spoon

these dried herbs

Dear Diary,
   Isn't it wonderful? All of my dreams are coming true! First I found my love, and tonight my restaurant is opening. With hard work and a little luck, anything is possible. Now I'm off to check on the gumbo. It surely smells good!

Tiana

Search and discover these things for food lovers:

photo

this menu

Grand Opening
banner

reservation book

lucky horseshoe   newspaper review

Dear Diary,
    I found another treasure from the human world today. My collection is growing! I wonder if I'll ever find out what it's like to live on land and walk on legs. Oh, well—a mermaid can dream!

Ariel

Find this selection from Ariel's collection:

hourglass

candelabra

dinglehopper

box of thingamabobs

this painting

pair of glasses

Dear Diary,
Today was the happiest day of my life by far! First I married my prince, and then we celebrated at a party with all our friends. I didn't know that Gus and Jaq could waltz. What a wonderful surprise!

Cinderella

Look end to end for Cinderella's friends:

Jaq

Luke

this bluebird

this bluebird

Bruno

Fairy Godmother

Gus

Suzy

Climb back up the tower to find these supplies for Rapunzel's greatest joy, painting:

In the happy ending of Belle's story, her enchanted friends become human again. Can you find their pictures in the castle?

Snow White's picnic has something tasty for everyone. Can you spot these delicious treats?

Thank goodness Aurora's fairies haven't turned *everything* pink! Fly back to the garden and look for these colorful animals: